The
King & the
Cuddly

To India - M.N.
To Peter - P.B.

A Red Fox Book

Published by Random House Children's Books
20 Vauxhall Bridge Road, London SW1V 2SA

A division of The Random House Group Ltd
London Melbourne Sydney Auckland
Johannesburg and agencies throughout the world

3 5 7 9 10 8 6 4 2

First published in Great Britain by Hutchinson Children's Books 2000
Red Fox edition 2000

Printed in Singapore by Tien Wah Press (PTE) Ltd

THE RANDOM HOUSE GROUP Ltd Reg. No. 954009
www.randomhouse.co.uk

The King & the Cuddly

MARJORIE NEWMAN

ILLUSTRATED BY
PETER BOWMAN

RED FOX

Once there was a forest.
Deep in the forest there was a cave.

And in the cave lived
Cuthbert the Strong.

Every day, Cuthbert marched through the
forest, bold and brave. As he went he roared,
'I'm the king of the forest! I'm the king of the forest!'

The other animals thought he was splendid.

But when he was tired,
Cuthbert went home,
had his bath ...

... and snuggled down
in bed with his secret cuddly.

One evening Cuthbert
was ready to snuggle
down when –
'**Oh!**' cried Cuthbert,
looking under his blanket.

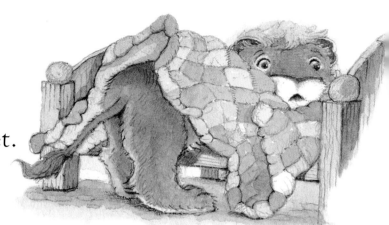

'**Ah!**' cried Cuthbert,
peeping under his pillow.

'**Help!**' cried Cuthbert,
whirling around to
search his cave.
'Where's my cuddly?'

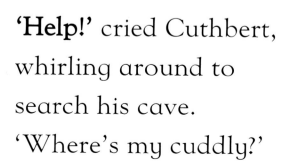

He couldn't find it.

Out into the
forest rushed Cuthbert.
'**Oh!**' cried Cuthbert,
searching among the trees.
'**Ah!**' cried Cuthbert, stumbling over the roots.
'**Help!**' cried Cuthbert, rushing around in all directions.
'Where's my cuddly?'
He *still* couldn't find it.

Along the river bank rushed Cuthbert.
'**Oh!**' cried Cuthbert, peering into a
crocodile's home.

'Ah!' cried Cuthbert, nearly tripping over
the crocodile (who unexpectedly was at home).

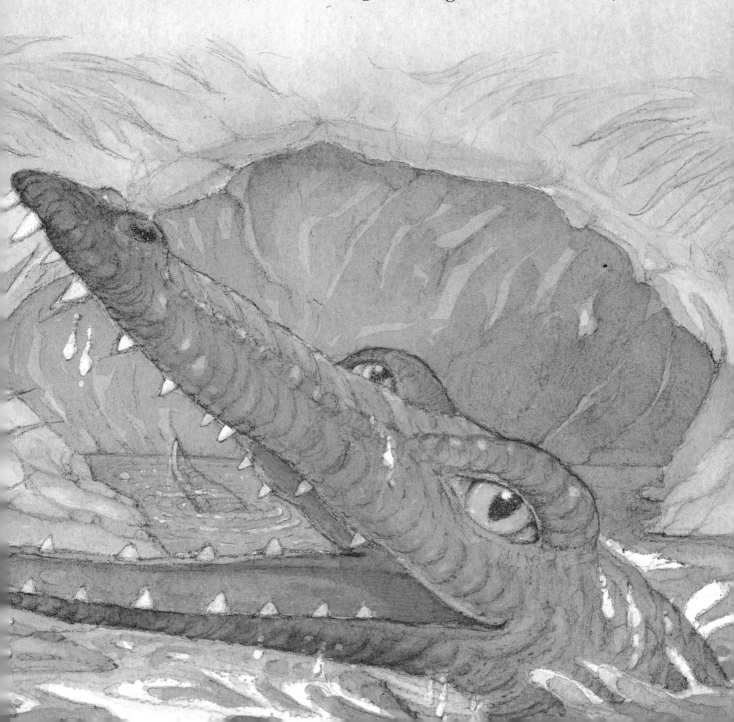

'**Help!**' cried Cuthbert, slipping into the
water with a tremendous splash.
'Where's my cuddly?'
It wasn't there.

Down the river went Cuthbert,
floating on an old tree trunk.

'Oh!' cried Cuthbert, as the tree went faster and faster.

'Ah!' cried Cuthbert, as the tree came closer and closer to the rocks.

'Help!' yelled Cuthbert, as the tree crashed amongst them and he flew through the air.

'Where's my cuddly?' he gasped, landing on the grass with a bump.

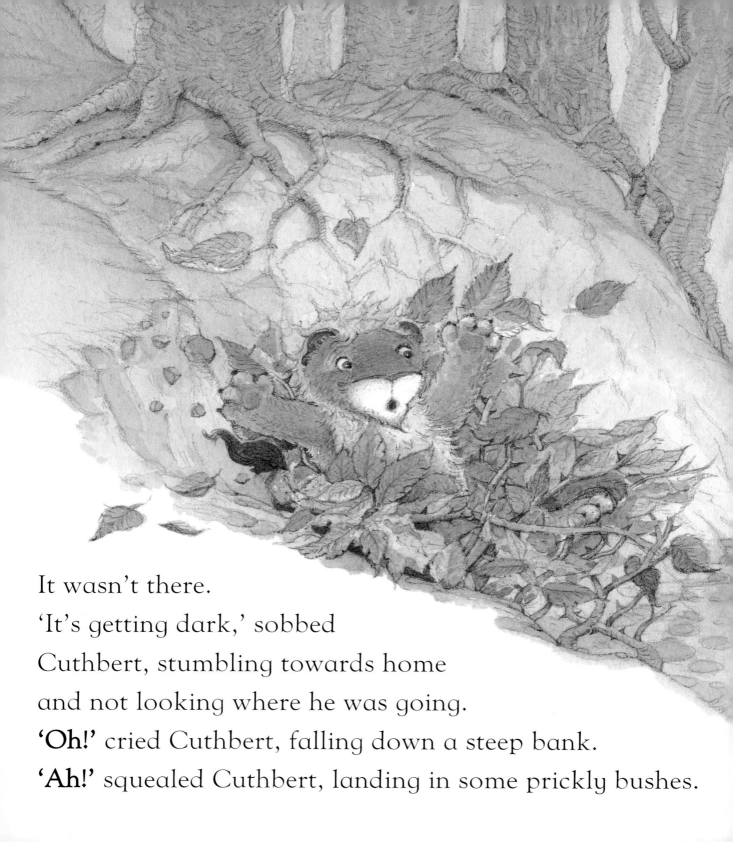

It wasn't there.
'It's getting dark,' sobbed
Cuthbert, stumbling towards home
and not looking where he was going.
'**Oh!**' cried Cuthbert, falling down a steep bank.
'**Ah!**' squealed Cuthbert, landing in some prickly bushes.

'**Help!**' shouted Cuthbert,
trying to get free ...

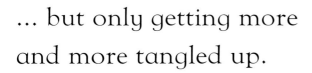

... but only getting more
and more tangled up.

'I'm stuck, and I haven't even
got my cuddly with me!'
The other animals heard him.
Cautiously they came to see
what was going on.

Carefully the animals rescued Cuthbert from the prickles.
Carefully they hauled him back up the bank. Secretly
the smallest mouse crept away to Cuthbert's cave.
'I can't find my cuddly anywhere!' sobbed Cuthbert.

'We'll help you,' said the other animals.
Just as they reached Cuthbert's cave, the smallest
mouse came out to meet them. 'Is this your cuddly,
Cuthbert?' she asked.
'Oh, yes, it is!' cried Cuthbert. 'Where did you find it?'
'It was under the bed,' smiled the mouse.

Cuthbert hugged his cuddly. Then his face went very red.

Now the other animals would know his secret.

But – 'Don't worry, Cuthbert!' said the other animals.

'Wait a minute!'

They raced to their homes and back again.
'Look!' they cried. 'We've all got cuddlies!'
'So we have!' smiled Cuthbert.

He went into his cave and snuggled down with
his not-so-secret-anymore cuddly.
'I don't feel big and strong all the time,' he admitted.
'Nobody does!' replied the other animals.
'Well, that's all right then,'
yawned Cuthbert.
He closed his eyes.

'But I'm still king of the forest,' he said sleepily.
'And tomorrow is another day!'

Some bestselling Red Fox picture books

THE BIG ALFIE AND ANNIE ROSE STORYBOOK
by Shirley Hughes
OLD BEAR
by Jane Hissey
JOHN PATRICK NORMAN McHENNESSY –
THE BOY WHO WAS ALWAYS LATE
by John Burningham
I WANT A CAT
by Tony Ross
NOT NOW, BERNARD
by David McKee
THE STORY OF HORRIBLE HILDA AND HENRY
by Emma Chichester Clark
THE SAND HORSE
by Michael Foreman and Ann Turnbull
BAD BORIS GOES TO SCHOOL
by Susie Jenkin-Pearce
MRS PEPPERPOT AND THE BILBERRIES
by Alf Prøysen
BAD MOOD BEAR
by John Richardson
WHEN SHEEP CANNOT SLEEP
by Satoshi Kitamura
THE LAST DODO
by Ann and Reg Cartwright
IF AT FIRST YOU DO NOT SEE
by Ruth Brown
THE MONSTER BED
by Jeanne Willis and Susan Varley
DR XARGLE'S BOOK OF EARTHLETS
by Jeanne Willis and Tony Ross
JAKE
by Deborah King